The Princess

the King

and the

Anarchist

The Princess

the King

and the

Anarchist

Robert Pagani

*Translated from
the French by
Helen Marx*

Helen Marx Books
New York

© 2008 by
Éditions de La Table Ronde, Paris

First English edition
© 2010 by Helen Marx Books

Library of Congress
Control Number: 2009943251

ISBN 978-1-9335-2720-8

FRONTISPIECE: *Arrival of Princess Ena at the Church for the Wedding of King Don Alfonso XIII of Spain and Victoria Eugenia of Battenberg in Madrid May 31, 1906*, by Apic. Getty Images.

Introduction

Caroline Weber

The king is a thing.

—WILLIAM SHAKESPEARE, *Hamlet*

On May 31, 1906, in Madrid, an anarchist named Mateo Morral tried to assassinate Spain's royal couple—King Alfonso XIII and his nineteen-year-old, English-born bride, Princess Mary Eugenia Victoria Battenberg—on their wedding day. Taking this episode as the point of departure for his début novel, the Swiss author Robert Pagani gives it an extraordinary spin by beginning the tale with these lines:

> The day she became queen, there were lots of flowers, lots of noises, lots of blood, and lots of dead bodies, but she wasn't particularly surprised. During the ten seconds that followed the explosion, she wasn't even very agitated, not be-

cause she was in shock but because her mind was somewhere else.

"She," of course, is the freshly minted Queen María Eugenia, as her new family and subjects have renamed her. And the blood and corpses referenced just after the posies and the cheers evoke the violence that intrudes so abruptly and improbably on her and Alfonso's carriage ride from the cathedral back to their palace. This juxtaposition—of flowers and dead bodies—is startling enough. But the real jarring note comes in the second sentence, with the observation that the attack doesn't even "surprise" her. This begs the obvious question: What subject so preoccupies María Eugenia that her would-be killer's bomb (disguised, in fact, in a bouquet of flowers he flings at the wedding procession) fails, initially, to penetrate the young queen's consciousness?

Penetration, it turns out, is exactly the issue, because in the moments following her marriage ceremony, as she and her husband are driven through throngs of cheering *madrileños*, the young woman's thoughts turn to sex. Like any royal bride of her era, María Eugenia is a virgin with only the vaguest sense of what her wedding night will entail. Later in the narrative, she writes, in a touchingly candid letter home:

This is the big night, dear Mummy, when I shall become both queen and wife. I so wish you were next to me, dear Mother, yes, next to me. I say what I feel. At least, in the next room. You must think that's absurd and ridiculous, but it's the truth. I'm so afraid of being clumsy.

Deprived of her mother's company and counsel, the young queen cannot stop herself from wondering what her sexual "congress"—a word she gleaned from a "forbidden" book glimpsed in a library back home—with handsome, sensual Alfonso will entail. This curiosity prompts a series of flashbacks (a glimpse of animals copulating in the barnyard at Balmoral) and fantasies (will Alfonso's member really be the size of "a large carrot," and if so, how will it ever fit into her "narrow orifice"?) so absorbing that even a murderer's bomb can't immediately disrupt her train of thought.

Just as strikingly, her musings about her and her husband's nether regions merge, over the course of the carriage ride, with an increasingly desperate need to urinate. "Pipi, always, pipi," she repeats to herself. "Pipi. It was beginning to be painful." This distinctly unmajestic term continues to punctuate the queen's interior monologue as the royal procession moves along its inexorable path toward the palace . . . and the murderer's bomb. Indeed, the latter makes its appearance just as María Eugenia has worked up the courage to tell her husband about her embarrassing plight.

Meanwhile, unbeknownst to his wife, Alfonso has been ruminating on his own, parallel discomfort. As Pagani's narrative point of view moves back and forth between the newlyweds (periodically shifting to the anarchist as well), the reader learns that Spain's august sovereign is suffering from an indomitable erection: "His rod, an erect mast in the middle of his body, is ebony, steel. What will he do if nothing changes? . . . He feels, around the erect baobab of his pubis, an intense, painful tingling." Like his bride, the king—riding through Madrid on one of the most sacred occasions of his reign—is consumed by impulses of the earthiest, most elemental kind.

In a story about the attempted destruction of a royal couple, this insight is far from incidental. On the contrary, the pair's insistent physicality underscores their profound vulnerability to the lurking antimonarchist threat. Although the bomb narrowly misses its targets, it leaves María Eugenia with gore splattered all over her wedding gown—and, once she begins to process what has transpired, with a heightened sense of her own fragility. ("A piece of living, torn, living, flesh is all she is," she reflects in a panic after the

fact.) Notwithstanding Alfonso's valiant protestations
to the contrary—"Come now, it's over. . . . Tomorrow
we'll go duck-hunting, and kings are eternal"—his
wife's baptism by blood, and his own shredded tunic,
give the lie to the fiction upon which European mo-
narchical rule has ever been founded: the idea, precisely, that the royal body transcends mortality.

As analyzed by the medieval historian Ernst Kantorowicz in his classic 1957 study, *The King's Two Bodies*, this myth holds that even as the sovereign's corpo-
real being is subject to injury, decay, and death, he is
possessed of a transcendental, mystical being that both
incarnates and subtends the body politic. According
to Kantorowicz, such a conception of the kingly body
informs the seemingly paradoxical utterance "The
King is dead. Long live the King!" Perhaps a more
compelling example, however, lies in the seventeenth-
century French King Louis XIV's reaction to a gru-
eling hemorrhoid operation. After reviving from a
swoon into which the agony of the procedure had
plunged him, Louis announced to his anxious court-
iers: "The man is suffering, but the king is doing fine."
(Today, in twenty-first-century New York, María Eugenia's real-life nephew, Prince Dimitri of Yugosla-
via, loves to repeat this "family anecdote," which for
him stands as a supreme example of royal dignity and

gloire.) Like Louis's more celebrated pronouncement, "*l'état, c'est moi,*" this assertion of kingly immortality is the ideological bedrock of absolute monarchy.

Yet in Pagani's novel, the royal couple—whose sexual longings are expected to serve the interests of their dynasty—is confronted with a belief system that rejects their exalted status out of hand. Upheld by a mysterious stranger carrying a deadly bouquet, this system holds that "they must tumble! All those crowns, all those heads!" And although this anarchist —here identified only by the false name "Fernando" —does not succeed in his fatal quest, he scores an almost equally momentous victory against the institution that his would-be victims embody. In his flight from the police after flinging the bomb, "Fernando" winds up hiding in a shed in the palace gardens, where he encounters a dazed, disoriented María Eugenia. What ensues in their improbable, intimate tête-à-tête exposes the physical vulnerability (and the attendant political precariousness) of the princely caste as a whole.

Needless to say, no such encounter between a committed anarchist and a royal virgin figures in the actual historical record; nor do the cataclysmic events in which, following on the heels of the meeting in the shed, Pagani's story culminates. The real Mateo Morral committed suicide in prison two days after his botched assassination attempt. His imaginary counterpart meets a far more astonishing fate—at the hands of a young woman who, though the actions of "Fernando" undermine the fantasy of royal inviolability once and for all, is not quite ready to concede the point. The words with which *The Princess, the King, and the Anarchist* concludes, "He is the king," register less as an assertion of unflappable sovereign power than as a case of pathetic wishful thinking. In this respect, the anarchist succeeds where his bomb failed—by shaking the royal body, and soul, to their very foundations.

The Princess

the King

and the

Anarchist

T HE DAY SHE BECAME QUEEN, there were lots of flowers, lots of noises, lots of blood, and lots of dead bodies, but she wasn't particularly surprised. During the ten seconds that followed the explosion, she wasn't even very agitated, not because she was in shock but because her mind was somewhere else. Three months earlier, she had read a book, or, more precisely, only the first page of a book, since it had been taken away immediately, coming as it did from a shelf in the library forbidden to her; this book told the story of a music professor and his wife and began as follows:

The first time was in Calais, where the boat had dropped them off in the early evening, at a seedy little hotel in front of the harbor dock; sixty-two years later, the last time was in a village on Lake Maggiore, after a trip to Rome, and moreover, that one was fatal (for him). They had congress, in between, four thousand six hundred and twenty-three times (she kept count in a small sheepskin notebook; he, too, kept count, unbeknownst to her, in a small cardboard notebook). Almost all the congresses were successful. The two of them were never, from the beginning until the end, separated more than a day. Their life

1

was an oasis of quiet happiness that had nothing to do with boredom. Quite the contrary. Over the years, they had experienced harsh and dramatic events: a crime was even committed that first night under their window. A sailors' brawl went awry, and the following morning you could still see, on the sidewalk, the outlines of a large puddle of blood. Six months later, adjacent to their house in Saint-Martin-upon-Soames, a cattle dealer, who had overcelebrated his good trades at the fair, fell into a well, and . . .

She never was able to find out if the unfortunate fellow was able to climb out of the well in the Shropshire backwoods, but that was not important. "Congress" intrigued her. The dictionaries she consulted said nothing that corresponded to her vague sense of the word.

And that other word: "success." How could a congress be a success? This also implied failure. But the number was what really plunged her into deep thought: four thousand six hundred and twenty-three?

Could that be possible? Was it even conceivable?

You would think that twenty times in the course

of a life span, or twenty-five if one lived to be terribly old, would be considerable.

All these fuzzy thoughts floated around in her head; it was probably best to do what her cousin Emily and Princess Alice had counseled: don't brood and these matters will easily take care of themselves. So much in life brought one happiness—simple things, very simple things . . . A walk in the forest, a swim in the river, a game of backgammon, hide-and-seek in the woods around Balmoral Castle . . . Quite frankly, it wasn't worthwhile worrying about a side of life that was only one of many others and not even the most interesting at that.

3

He adored hunting. Everywhere on his visit to England, at Cornwall Grounds, Hampton, Sandringham, and then at the Duke of Devon's (dear Uncle Terry), he had amazed the whole family, even the Prince of Wales, great connoisseur, with his ability. He had a good eye and quick hands. At just twenty he had better anticipation than most experienced hunters. Few pheasants escaped his bullets. She loved him.

His profile stood out against the teeming brightness of the street. The face was well proportioned, with a high forehead and a handsome, not very bourbony nose. The whole effect was, thank goodness, definitely more Bourbon than Hapsburg. He took after his father rather than his mother, who had inherited a hint of her ancestors' receding chin.

The procession advanced slowly to an irregular but pleasant sound on the large cobblestones. Independence Plaza was at the end of the avenue. There, they would circle the monument and head for Alcalá Street toward the Puerta del Sol. Queen of Spain! My God . . . She was actually queen of Spain!

She knew nothing about Spain, except that England owned a small piece of it, and spoke only about a dozen words of the language. She would learn. They said the grammar wasn't too difficult. The worst part was conjugating the verbs.

"There," he said, taking her hand, "is the Buen Retiro." Something happened to her when he held her hand.

The procession slowed down even more, to a walk. The crowds on the sidewalk screamed with joy.

"It's for you," he said. "You, María Eugenia, are what they applaud."

"Oh! But surely it must be especially for you!" she said. "You are their king."

Was he loved by his people? Apparently so. Grandmother V. used to say, "It's important that they respect us." Certainly, but love, too, mattered between subjects and kings. It had to be better when it did exist. If the king of France had been more loved, would the people have cut off his head?

Just a short time ago, she had been only one candidate among eight others, seven with nobler blood than hers, since a small portion of hers was not noble. He had chosen her, in spite of this blot on her lineage. He had met her first and could easily have forgotten her by the time he reached the end of the list. "But," he had said to her, "the others were just a formality to please my mother." His mother, in fact, did not like the idea of an alliance with the English. "Nothing good for Spain ever comes out of England." He had laughingly repeated this remark on the day of their engagement.

More than merely attraction, it could have been love at first sight with any of the other seven. But it wasn't, and now she was no longer Mary, but María, María Eugenia Victoria.

The monarchist newspaper had submitted a question to its readers: "Who will be the next queen of Spain?" The British embassy had communicated the results to Mother. Mother didn't show them to her, but she had seen the telegram on her desk. So as not to be caught spying, she copied the text quickly. Of the eight highly born princesses, four, including three of her cousins, were English, three German, and one

French. She had won the most votes—18,427—compared to 13,719 for her cousin Patricia, and 10,765 for Louise d' Orléans. It was rumored the king had a particular preference for her, but in any case, his decision was already made. "From the very first minute." And what about her? What about her heart? Since when? The first minute too? Yes.

Oh God, this carriage is taking forever! It reminded her of a story she'd read as a child. The king of a tiny kingdom had only one carriage, about as speedy as a snail. Because of this, he took too long to go and fetch his fiancée, who tired of waiting and married another king. He wasn't rich, either, and the two little kings waged war with tiny weapons.

Could she hold out? Standing before the archbishop in church, she already had wanted to go. Had she known this would take so long, at the end of the ceremony she would have asked to be excused for a few minutes. Or asked for a chamber pot. A chamber pot! My God! What wouldn't she think of next, on a day like today! And, on top of everything else, she, a native of the country that had invented flush toilets!

"The War Ministry is down there, at the end of the avenue, behind those big trees."

Many wars had been fought between England and Spain. Now they would stop.

He took her hand again and brought it to his lips. Yesterday he had kissed her on the cheek. He smelled of tobacco, but good tobacco, from Cuba or the Philippines, those beautiful colonies Spain had just lost. She, too, smoked. Mother and Madame Mère disapproved but said nothing. What could they say to someone who now took precedence over them. Madame Mère was not easy. It would be hard at the beginning. "If things don't go well," Uncle Edward (no longer her king) had said, "you can't come back here sniveling." Harsh words, but meant to give her courage.

Uncle Edward, king of England and emperor of India, was good to her. He had greatly supported Mother when Father, going off to get himself killed in Africa, had turned her into a widow responsible for a family.

At moments the snail-like procession became turtle-like. It moved forward in fits and starts. Maybe because of the crowd that, here and there, broke through the barriers to better see their long-awaited new queen. "We are two orphans," he had said in Biarritz when he came to ask Mummy for her hand in marriage. His father had died before he was born. King in his mother's belly. Actually born a king in the history books and proud of his uniqueness.

Aunt Alice had said to keep her legs straight. But how could she? Cunningly, she had managed to consult a medical book in a small office off the library at Balmoral. In the chapter on obstetrics, the anatomical illustrations were either too explicit or not explicit enough. Stretched out, really straight . . . no, it just wasn't possible. The thing wasn't placed well enough for that. It depended on the other things and the way it tilted, but . . . no . . . too low. Curiously low. Maybe to protect it. Well, that's the way it was. When you thought about it, nature certainly was curious.

Was he experienced? Still so young . . . so fresh, so childlike . . . Maybe Princess Alice had consciously told her only a part of the truth so as not to frighten her?

For some time, another term besides *congress* had been churning around in her head. Two years earlier, walking behind the stables at Windsor, she had inadvertently overheard the grooms talking. *Legs in the air* was one of the expressions they had used. Legs in the air? What did that expression relate to? Was it a kind of horsemanship? That didn't seem quite right. Did it refer to a proverb? But the men were laughing lewdly, so it made one think of something not quite decent. Until that evening, she suddenly saw women's legs raised all over the place: in the rose garden, in the formal salon, at the dining room table, sitting between the king and queen of England. But why women? Well, yes, certainly.

Those same legs—hers, what a horror!—now shot up at the carriage windows, above all those sheep-like faces. They were white and straight. Was that what Princess Alice, her dear aunt, had wanted to say? Oh! How she would still love to talk to her, if only about this, and be able to ask questions! Impossible by telegram. By letter—too late, way too late.

Pipi, always, pipi. Think about something else. Golf. She had taught him the basics, and by the third day he was already better than she. He grasped it all very quickly. He was one of those fortunate people who know things before the fact: how to make an omelette, tie a sailor's knot, drive a car. He was so different from her original impression, which was based on what they had told her: wild man, practical joker, smoker. Spain was lucky. And so was she.

The great organ of Saint Geronimo still rang in her ears. She had been so happy. She had never been happier in her life than at that moment, in spite of the tiresome urge that had already arisen. The music enveloped her like a soft cashmere shawl, like her mother's body when she had told her about Papa's death at the hands of the savages. She didn't regret having embraced Catholicism, although she'd had a lot of difficulty pronouncing the necessary words! After all, she had had to repudiate *her* religion.

She repeated the words in front of the mirror, trying to empty her mind and simply mouth them by rote. "With a sincere heart, I detest and abhor all error, all heresy, and any sect contrary to the word of the Catholic, Apostolic, and Roman Church."

She was Protestant Anglican, as were her family and her country. Now she had a new country and belonged to another nation. "Passionate, irresponsible, and wild," Uncle James had said. But aren't all nations passionate, and isn't it the role of their king to dominate and channel those passions? She would do whatever she possibly could to make herself loved by him. Anything and everything.

At Balmoral, she had seen a boar coupling with a sow. It was easier for animals. You could say their physical makeup made them better suited to each other. Emily had talked about instinct and how that was what mattered most during the act. Instinct being the expression and instrument of a great vital force. A black curtain fell. Reason grew dim. During this lapse, bodies reached out together in harmony and claimed their own solutions. At thirteen, trying to cross a gate, she had briefly found herself astride a beam and experienced an unknown, violent, and fleeting sensation that bothered her until teatime. She never said a word to anyone, not even to Mummy, who might have enlightened her. She didn't experience the sensation again, even on horseback. Emily had alluded to it, and she should have asked for details then, but maybe she was afraid to learn the answer. Somehow, she felt, a disturbing world loomed "out there." Would this world be unveiled tonight? She was frightened.

"And the big pink building is the Ministry of Finance, where I have never set foot. I should, too."

Be unveiled. By this man, sitting beside her, who was still terra incognita.

"We are about to arrive at the Puerta del Sol. Do you remember, darling, I spoke about it?"

"Yes."

"It's the heart of Madrid." He pronounced it "Madri." So that's how you say it.

Once again, the choral voices burst within her clear and fresh. Oh, yes, she would be happy. Ministerial functionaries crowded at windows. The procession was now passing under triumphal arches, nearer and nearer to each other. The mob shouted their names. The women's eyes glistened with tears. She would have liked to embrace them all: young and old, peasants with roughened cheeks, darkened by the harsh Spanish sun. The carriage in front of them carried Madame Mère and her two daughters. A yellow gloved arm would emerge to salute the crowd from time to time.

She might not ever see her mother again. The trip was so long and Mummy didn't like to travel. Maybe she would come for the birth of her first child. She preferred to not even think about the stomach that suddenly starts to swell, then unswells, only to swell again. Grandmother V.: nine times. But what if it didn't swell—not even once? Oh, Mary, don't be so stupid!

In Biarritz, after his proposal, they had gone out to run on the beach. She could still feel the sand, firm and soft under her feet. Facing the sea, they had gazed out at the horizon. He had turned his head and stared at her breasts for a long time. She had hunched forward in order to hide them.

At the Puerta del Sol, the route climbed and then descended, then it seemed to climb once again, endlessly. The procession entered, unhurried, into the Calle Mayor. Now it wasn't very far. It would be a five-minute walk. She always won, at Balmoral, when her cousins decided to race from the end of the avenue to the bottom of the steps. As soon as the carriage had cleared the palace walls, she would make it stop, in spite of disrupting ceremonial protocol, and like this, just as she was in her white dress, gloves, and crown of flowers, she would run. Too bad about the arrangements, too bad for Spain, too bad for England, she would run between a double row of soldiers, who had aligned themselves in quick formation and would hide her behind their backs, until they reached the nearest toilet. Maybe that of the guardsmen, where a queen had never before entered.

His best years had been in Barcelona. That's when he had understood everything. The reality of things. The meaning of life. The organization of society. His great strength. Men's lives were not what one thought. As he looked at the crowds in the street, on the Ramblas, at first he saw just a dark mass; then, lines drawn with cracks and breaks; full spaces and empty spaces formed as individuals became separate, one from another. Like different bodies in a chemical reaction, each had a particular shape and special characteristics. That was only an illusion. They were all the same, all encased in their binding corsets until the corsets were the only things he could distinguish: hundreds of upright corsets, jostling each other anonymously, side by side, in abject submission.

He had tried to explain this to his mother and brothers, but they hadn't understood a word. Neither had his sisters. Neither had Pedro, his cousin, who was, nevertheless, intelligent, who read newspapers and even books.

"What corsets, Fernando?"

"Let's say their prison."

"Their prison?"

Occasionally, Mother became exasperated. "You're the one who'll end up in prison if you go on filling your head with ideas like that!"

It wasn't even worth trying with Uncle Juan or Uncle Epifanio or with Aunt Cecilia, who was born wearing a corset and would die, mummified, still wearing it. He could have talked to Papa about them. If society were more just, his father would not be dead. He had tried, only once. He had hurled the question, like a stone, at his mother: "And Father, why did he die, huh?"

The answer had disarmed him: "Why do you ask that? You know very well. He slipped." Yes, he had slipped. In a mine where men worked twelve-hour shifts with no security measures.

Ferrer used to repeat again and again, "Family is the main hindrance." Family is the biggest calamity. Some people didn't agree. Without family, you have nothing. "Without family, you have it all," he would answer.

"It's nature's law."

"Nature's law, pfft!"

"Nevertheless, Antonio, in the beginning, no matter what kind of organism you have, there is a cell."

"Maybe. But only temporarily. Ultimately, it's an impermanent simple biological phenomenon that changes nothing."

15

Ferrer opposed the organic development of that cell. "Neither family nor nation" was his motto, his religion. He didn't realize it, himself, back then. Had worried the question at length and left the city to think about it even more. In Aragon, he had walked for days, sleeping in barns, chased by peasants' dogs. Dirty, starved, exhausted. Sitting on a hill, at the edge of a forest, he contemplated the fields, the bowed backs of the tillers, the working horses, the children of the petite bourgeoisie on their way to school, the children of the dockhands not on their way, families celebrating some event—baptism, marriage—under a tree. Their songs and their carousals created, too, a kind of happiness. "An unconscious happiness," Antonio said. "Yes, but . . . "

"A brutish happiness, but it's all the same. The peasants will come last. First, the cities."

Princess Maria Antonia had a special something. He felt a shiver down his spine when she leaned slightly out of the box to signal a friend in the orchestra. He was madly in love. His opera glasses devoured her. She, too, adjusted hers. Her head swiveled. Sometimes the binoculars met and stayed suspended, like two foreign creatures assembled in parallel waves that nature carried toward each other. That made them laugh. She did have an easy laugh, Princess Maria Antonia von Mecklenburg-Schwerin. Then something bizarre happened: the next day, the shiver was gone, as though a kind of champagne tipsiness had evaporated suddenly.

In the silence of the little rococo palace put at his disposal during the stay, every morning he stared at the ceiling and systematically and logically compared the two princesses. The Englishwoman won out in the end and regained her place of honor. He had written to her but not yet received an answer. Had the letter been lost? She knew he was in Germany, but Germany is big. It reaches way out as far as the limits of the Russian plains.

He was anxious to return to France. He only liked one thing about Germany—the cuisine: potatoes and sausages. That was his Habsburg side, so it was a given. He hated long meals and elaborate dishes. A snack on horseback meant as much to him as the grandest dinner.

Mother would have wanted him to choose an Austrian princess. "Back to your roots," she used to say. Answer: "Mother, my heart will decide." Could he tell her his heart had already decided? He had to leave as little time as possible for her to develop her usual schemes. He had written to England to tell his pretty blonde princess (no wheat could be blonder) that he would be at Pau "with Henry IV." She was familiar with the story and knew that Henry's libertine blood also flowed in his. At Henry's old castle in Pau, there was yet another princess, this one French: Louise Orléans. Did Mary know she existed? Would she be jealous? Did she already love him enough to feel pangs of jealousy?

When he arrived in Madrid, it was bitterly cold. He had only a vest and, to keep from dying, had stolen for the first time. He had grabbed the coat from its hanger in an old junk shop and run. People ran after him screaming and as soon as he closed his eyes, he could hear their voices. Stop, thief! Stop, thief! Later, because he had to eat, he stole again. After that, Ferrer had sent him money.

Madrid was horrible. He walked endlessly, down infinitely long avenues, hemmed in by huge dark buildings. Walking: occupation of the poor. Buen Retiro was the only place he felt all right. He read the paper on a bench, eating nuts. Little old men spoke to him. The backwardness of Spain and of the world rested on their deformed shoulders, and he felt like insulting them.

To clean. To purify. First order of business.

It was a sign that spring had come early. The shrubs and trees were already shedding their flowers. The rain enhanced their perfumes. He went to a brothel. Ferrer would not have been pleased to learn he was wasting the movement's money this way. The girl, a thick and ugly Austrian, had immediately opened her legs and turned her head away. It reminded him of rotten fruit with decomposing pulp. He hadn't felt a thing and returned in a rage to the pension.

The pension was kept by an old couple and cost him twenty-five pesetas a day. The husband did the cooking. The daughter, a sad and dry long drink of water, served the meals wordlessly. He tried to imagine her hardened and shrunken genitals. The other boarders were small-time workers who resembled her: corseted, gray, and taciturn. Their threadbare clothes swallowed them up, and they polished their own shoes. Bachelors. Separated. Rejected. Was it worth saving humanity? That humanity. Ignobly humble and downtrodden. Ferrer didn't like those kinds of questions and swept them away dismissively. "A doctor doesn't ask himself if it's worth saving a sick person. He simply makes the effort."

It was hot. Too hot. The *madrileños* had a saying to describe their climate: "Six months of winter, six months of hell." He walked. The next morning, his shirt was still drenched with sweat. He smelled terrible. His money would just about hold out. At noon, he ate an apple in a park and then nothing until evening. He drank a glass of wine before going in for dinner. He had hooked a calendar next to his beaten-up bed. He counted the days.

She wouldn't see her cousins again! How she would miss Timothy! Dear Tim! He was the funniest of them all. Always full of ideas for games, pranks, and crafty schemes. He used to race with his dogs and always won because he knew how to pace himself and they didn't. At sixteen, she thought she'd fallen in love, even though she didn't know then what love was. Did she know any better now? Mummy's explanation: "To feel good next to him, without looking at him or saying a word." Grandmother V. didn't think anything at all. No one had ever heard her talk about feelings. According to her, duty came before all else. The rest was incidental. For her darling new king, pleasure came first. The embassy had sent along information on the subject. One of his favorite diversions was to leave the palace incognito, at night, and wander around the streets of Madrid. In Paris, visiting the president of the Republic, he had embraced a flower seller in the market. His attendants did not appreciate this foolishness and his mother hated it.

They endeavored to have him meet only official persons, but it was difficult to curb him. He slipped out of their hands like an eel. He adored driving himself and just this morning had come to fetch her in a sixty-horsepower Panhard 50. It was hard to believe, but the rumor was that once on the road to Aranjuez he had pushed the motor to seventy kilometers an hour.

Four thousand six hundred and twenty-three. Was it possible? When an heir was produced, what was the point? Besides that, if you thought about it, it was basically disgusting. One time, walking down the west wing at Sandringham, strange cries she had never heard before rang out. How to describe them? Not really of suffering and yet . . . like suffering but without the pain. Could it be Aunt Gwendolyn? Her baby was due at the end of the month, but occasionally nature pushed matters forward. In those cases, women suffered in childbirth; Mummy had suffered terribly giving birth to her, the youngest. This, however, seemed like something else altogether: these were very special cries, almost of happiness.

Where did he go on his nocturnal outings? Did he have companions in his debauchery? Like Uncle Edward, gossips said, the dear king of England, and so many others.

She loved his smile, but the fact that it could disappear in the fraction of a second was strange. Just as a cloud out of nowhere can hide the sun. Someone, she didn't remember who, had said Bourbon became Habsburg.

Pipi. It was beginning to be painful.

Farms and fields and vineyards surrounded the Duchess of Alba's pretty little chateau. Young women worked in these vineyards. He sat down on a low wall. Some of them smiled. Did they know he came from the chateau and who he was under his disguise? That evening, one of them approached and dragged him behind the barn. Summer's heat seeped from the beams. She smelled heavily of sweat. In the blink of an eye, she was naked. The next instant, uttering a hoarse cry, she had opened herself up like a fruit and sucked him into her like a whirlpool. All right! That was it. That was really it, and it was done. As she left him, buttoning up her blouse, and looking deep into his eyes, she had smiled a sly smile. "I know who you are," it seemed to say.

They had searched for him, and Mother was furious. They would punish those responsible for letting him out. Fourteen! Anything could have happened: there were wolves around the area, as well as highway robbers.

He counted while the carriage entered the Calle Mayor. Twenty-five, twenty-six, twenty-seven. Maybe twenty-eight. Three in three hours before the president's official dinner in Paris. In Pau, the same one, three days running. She, the fresh new queen, would be number twenty-nine. Could he ever bring himself to tell her? He burst out laughing.

"What's so funny?"

"A woman in the crowd a while ago," he answered, "wearing a hat in the shape of a parrot. I thought at first he was real, that he would fly away and come here, into the carriage."

He took her hand again. With his gloved one, he caressed her arm, covered in organdy. He would have liked to feel her skin. His wife, his queen had milk-white, translucent English skin. He had only known dark skin, except in Germany. An awkward, big woman, she took forever to spread out and then, suddenly arching her back, had engulfed him. White and smooth. White and smooth, like her, his lovely queen.

Another thing he could never tell her. Life was full of things you couldn't repeat.

Oh, my God! Not that! If he was already hard at eleven ten, how could he last until evening? And, on top of everything, there was that deuced ball. He hated balls. They bored him to death. If you could dance on horseback maybe. But on a floor . . . no sense in that.

23

The square in front of the church swarmed with guards, policemen, and soldiers. The palace people were agitated and easily recognizable because they changed so quickly from arrogance to obsequiousness. In one moment their chests were bursting with self-importance; seconds later they were groveling on the ground. The one advantage to this: it was easier to go unnoticed in the crowd.

"What the hell are you doing here? You don't have the right to be here! Get out!"

"But the people also have the right to be at their king's wedding."

"Don't argue."

"He's the king of Spain, all Spain . . ."

"There's the gallery, but it's impossible here."

"Where do you have to go to reach the gallery?"

"Over there, on the left. But it's already full and there's hardly any room."

"If it's full, I'll come back down," he said submissively.

Ahead of him, men were climbing the spiral staircase, worn down through the centuries. The gallery opened up on the fourth floor. He was going to be pushed back before reaching it. In that case, he'd go down like a good little boy. Everything in its own time: he was still climbing. His heart beat like a drum against his ribs. Was it effort or emotion?

A sign indicated that the gallery was reserved for journalists. He took a notebook out of his pocket to mislead the person in charge, but no one asked him a question; he threaded himself deftly through the crowd and reached the parapet. The parapet was marble, carved in the Italian style, with fine hexagonal handrails and capitals in a vegetable motif. Before meeting Ferrer, he had tried to enroll in a fine arts academy, but that kind of school wasn't for people like him. Furthermore, and most especially, art was dangerous because it distracted from the sole mission of a man worthy of the name.

Directly below, the nave was filling up with women in beautiful dresses and gaudy-looking men splashed with epaulettes. The golden altar sparkled and teemed with churchmen in chasubles.

It was amusing to watch them from on high, all

these great personages so sure of their God-given rights, steeped in their own importance with their bald heads and wrinkled necks. Haughty and overweening, yet pitifully vulnerable. At the entrance to the church, uniformed men strove to keep the way clear for the wedding. Five after ten. The future couple couldn't be much longer now.

Pipi! Pipiiiiii! Ooooh!

The hurrahs intensified! The Spanish people loved their active, smart, young king. And now he was introducing them to the queen his heart had chosen, whom he had gone to find in the misty northland. A queen he had not yet kissed, only once touched lightly with his lips, just as protocol demanded. How he hated protocol. In Biarritz, she, the queen, had stolen away. He hadn't insisted. It was on the large terrace facing the ocean, amid the crashing waves.

He was erect right now, in the most shameful way, worse than a donkey in spring. If the hardness didn't subside, it would become annoying. Very, very annoying, given that it was not yet noon and the ball was not scheduled before ten.

Long live the King! Long live the King!

One night he had gotten lost and had to ask directions to the palace from a passerby. The unknown man had eyed him suspiciously: what business did that young fop have in the royal palace at three in the morning?

"It's so funny, you look like the king," he had exclaimed. "Maybe you've already been told that." She had laughed a little uncertainly when he told her the story. Was his pretty queen extremely attached to convention?

How irritating, this procession that inched forward like an accordion. Later, there would be the meal, then the gossiping and then the preparations for the ball and then God knows what, another meal—people only thought about eating—and then the ball. And then and then and then. Unless he were a saint, how could a man be patient for so long? "There, behind, is the Plaza Mayor. That means big square. It's very beautiful. You haven't seen it yet?"

"No, you will show it to me."

"Of course. I'll help you discover Madrid with all its secret corners. The city is amazing, and slightly frightening too."

"Frightening? Why?"

"I don't know. She's proud; perhaps too much so."

"It won't be easy. They'll recognize us."

"We'll be disguised! I'll be a newsboy and you'll be a flower girl with a basket!"

She smiled. There was little laughter in her family. Just like in the Spanish family, under the regency of the stepmother. Happily, the old woman was dead. It was even worse, then, in England. Heavens, the things she thought about Grandmother V.! Should she go to confession now that she was Catholic . . . ?

A woman's existence consisted of a series of shocks that she forgot accordingly. Childbirth shattered her and, the next minute, she forgot the whole thing. God had given her this faculty. The God of Catholics was also the God of Protestants. There was only one God for every creature, all of whom were in his power. He had masterminded their mode of renewal and perpetuation. But why so big, the instrument, oh Lord? Emily had specified: like a medium-sized carrot, five to five and a half inches. No, not medium-sized but large, a large carrot. And the orifice was so narrow! It got bigger: the flesh down there was unbelievably expandable. "Do you realize, Mary, how expandable in order for an eight-pound baby to go through?" But even so, a large carrot was hard to believe. Wouldn't shorter and skinnier have been better? Did the seed need that kind of bulk to pass? Or rather, did God want women to suffer? But why? What had she done to deserve such punishment? "But, no, you little idiot, stop imagining these ideas!"

Emily had a rough side, which came from the Argylls, but which was proof of her sincerity. Before her marriage, she had wanted to see. "See what?"

"What do you mean, Mary?" Of course, she was so stupid. "I was, after all, the interested party!" It wasn't, anyhow, a condition she set because the marriage was decided, but ... Documentary evidence. It seems her fiancé, Prince Rupert, had laughed. He found his fiancée delightful. Initially, he demurred. "Everything in good time, darling." But Emily was stubborn. When she had an idea in her head, nothing made her give it up. Also, lest one forget, she had a healthy dose of Saxe-Coburg blood in her veins. She repeated her request. Demanded. If he had refused persistently, she might have been led to ask questions. Finally, he gave in. He turned the light down, so neither of them would feel embarrassed. The problem, however, was double-edged. Or, in other words, the thing could have two aspects. Emily hadn't thought of that. Its state at rest was hardly comparable to its extended one when ready for action. When she saw the later stage, she hadn't really been frightened but rather had trouble believing it could reach that size. But mainly, why? Half that size would already have seemed considerable and largely sufficient. "I told my-self, it was going to hurt me horribly. He made a face when I brought it up, as if to say that since the world began, billions of women had received said object with no particular damage to themselves."

She had also questioned Veronica, who had married the previous year. Veronica was the opposite of Emily: timid and fearful. She had blushed terribly. "You'll see, Mary," she murmured . . . before adding the next day in passing, "Just a bit, Mary. Don't be afraid. You must have faith in nature."

Just a bit what? What did she mean? That it hurt just a bit? Or that just a little entered? But a little or a lot, what did it matter with that amount of thickness? In a spirit of harmony, God had foreseen it all. Emily regretted having insisted, having seen. She had spent the last three weeks riddled with anxiety.

Just a bit . . . But were men all exactly the same? Conceived according to the same model? Shaped from the same pattern? Maybe his was less thick than the others? All the same! For a passage with hardly enough room for your little finger, even three times smaller would still be excessive.

"Yes, my beauty, with a basket!"

"But Madame Mère would never allow it."

"She won't know a thing. Needless to say, we won't tell her anything. And I am, after all, the king. And you, now, are the queen. You, my beauty, my love. We'll do what we please, you and I. We'll arrange things our own way. If you want to grow tomatoes in the grand salon, you shall!"

"Tomatoes? But . . . "

"Tomatoes, bananas, potatoes, carrots, everything!"

At the word *carrot*, she had shuddered. No, it wouldn't be easy, at the start! She was awfully Habsburg, Madame Mère. Queen mother, she was still queen. More queen than mother, she was feared. Her son also feared her. They would have to toe the line.

"Just a bit, and then you won't think about it, Mary. Afterwards, it's only happiness. Everything."

What everything?

The Calle Mayor seemed infinite. The palace was at the end, on the right. Maybe there was a toilet in the first building. There had to be. While the carriages finished pulling up to the curb, she would run with the youngest and slimmest of Madame Mère's ladies-in-waiting. Let them think what they pleased, and, in any case, they would pretend not to see. But without the train; the train risked catching everywhere and it would be simply impossible. Also, how could she lower her panties with all those pleats? Someone had to help her remove it. Oh! Dear God! Would she have time? She should have taken it off before getting into the carriage.

"What are you doing, darling?"

"The train. I should like to remove it."

"Remove it? Yes, of course. But now? Here? You'll have all the time in the world later, surely. You'll go rest and change before the meal, slowly, in the Spanish manner. Anyway, we're arriving soon. You see, we're already at number 48."

"How many are there in total?"

"Of numbers? I don't know, but less than a hundred. The palace is there, just behind. And it doesn't matter. It doesn't matter because I love you."

Leaning forward, he was suddenly very frightened. He was furious at having felt that fear. "Our only weapon is courage. They have power and all that goes with it: the police, the army, the clergy, everything. But they are cowards. It's their Achilles heel. Jellyfish! We, their opponents, have nothing except what they lack. Thanks to courage, we shall overcome."

The bride was already entering the nave on the arm of some prince, since her father was dead. He started counting to ten and had reached six when guards burst into the gallery. For him, he was certain. To seize him. Someone had denounced him; but who, since he knew no one? The game was up. "The prince!" they cried. "The prince! The Prince of Asturias!"

The Prince of Asturias! He was four years old, the Prince of Asturias! Four years old, an entourage surrounding him. The gallery was reserved only for him, so that he might follow a ceremony he didn't understand, and which would bore him to death; but which later would compose a paragraph in the story of his life. For this alone, he needed to be there.

The journalists found themselves below, discontent but obliged to keep quiet because the ceremony had started; even outside, behind the closed doors, silence had to be observed.

Once again, he had been lucky. As he had been a while ago to enter. No one had asked him anything: the guards, the police, the soldiers had other business. Good. Now he had plenty of time. He could walk peacefully back up the Calle del Prado, then from the Calle de Atocha to the Plaza Mayor, and then to the Calle Mayor. If that was inaccessible due to the imminent arrival of the procession, he'd go behind it. He was right to have moved out. First, he'd spent a few days at an old lady's near Lavapies. And then . . . by chance! Ferrer could talk all he wanted, but chance counted. Would he ever have dreamt of finding a place on the Calle Mayor? Directly on the Calle Mayor and on a high floor.

Until then, life had not indulged him. His father beat him. He hadn't shed a tear when he died. His mother preferred his sisters. One wondered if he was not the product of an adulterous affair she regretted. The only girl he had known left him after three months. A succession of bosses had all mistreated him. Indeed, they were only acting out their roles and conforming to the system. More reasonable ones had to exist, but he had only encountered the violent and the grasping. He would have liked to talk to someone else about his luck, his unbelievable luck, but he knew no one.

33

Not here, nor anywhere else. He would probably never see his family again. No brothers or sisters, uncles, aunts, or cousins. Ferrer, a prisoner of his own convictions, was indifferent to material things, and even more so to feelings. Only ideas counted in his eyes, and the result of their implementation. What was picturesque and subordinate interested him only fleetingly, even when the result was attained. His last resort was to look randomly in a huge city like Madrid, to randomly select a boardinghouse and then discover that it was on the route of the procession.

This represented a series of such miraculous strokes of fortune that he almost regretted not believing in God. He would have liked to express his gratitude to Him.

"Are you a monarchist, Fernando?" Mrs. Rodríguez had asked him.

"I love my king," he had responded.

"How fortunate! We do, too. It was not announced that the procession would pass by here, under our very windows. We hadn't given it a thought because, initially, the route was to have been up and down the Calle del Arsenal, there and back. So you can imagine how thrilled we were to hear that, instead, the procession would return to the palace by Mayor. It was totally unexpected! My husband was mad with joy and my daughter, too; the first time I have seen her smile in three years."

"I also am very happy, Señora."

"Ah, so much the better! Even though my husband holds, or had, rather socialistic ideas. I must say, though, ever since managing the boardinghouse again, he has changed; there are still traces of those ideas, but ideas or not, the king is always the king. Also, his grandfather was employed at court during Isabella II's reign and his father was an equerry at La Granja. That's not nothing. Finally, a king of Spain doesn't marry every day, right? Do you realize we saw his father's wedding procession, and my grandfather saw Isabella's in 1846. Don't you agree, it's almost like . . . like our own family?" She had laughed at her own boldness.

"Yes," he had said, "you're right, Mrs. Rodríguez."

"The royal family belongs to all Spaniards, is that not so?"

"Absolutely."

And, laughing again, she had added, "I gave you a good price, Fernando. I could have asked double: imagine, a room with a balcony for twenty-five pesetas! What a gift!"

"I realize that, only I could not have paid double or even ten pesetas more. Then you would have deprived a poor young man of perhaps his life's greatest happiness. You have acted generously. Doesn't that count, too?"

"True. That does matter." And suddenly she put her arms around him with tears in her eyes.

So narrow, yes, yes, yes, so narrow. My God! So tight. Barely the little finger! Was that normal? Was she normal? Emily, the index. Veronica, the thumb. But Veronica had hurt as much as Emily. She would be hurt, but he even more so. She didn't want him to be in pain because of her, her king, her beloved! No, not today of all days!

Certain streets were, in effect, blocked off: the Calle Atocha at the crossroads. Still carrying his big bouquet, he was obliged to head for the Calle de la Concepción.

He was already tired, having walked so much before now. When, abruptly—this certainly was a day of marvels!—an extraordinary lightness ballooned within him. He had never felt anything similar: at each step, as he placed his foot down, he honestly thought he would take off, rise in the air, and fly over the roofs in the sky of Madrid, above the arid Castilian plains.

He had never felt such happiness. A passerby saw the joy on his face.

"The procession doesn't pass by here," he said.

"I know," answered Fernando. "I'm turning at the corner."

"You must hurry, then. According to the program, it should appear any minute."

"Yes! I'll run! Good-bye!"

An extreme happiness almost unknown to the human condition prevented his breathing.

Back from his "princess tour," as the Duke of Medina-Campomayor said, he decided to play a practical joke on his mother and the Spanish people. He announced that he would paint the name of the chosen one on the prow of his yacht. Instead, he substituted a large question mark, which appeared on the front page of all the newspapers. He mentioned nothing about this to María Eugenia; she might have asked herself questions, since he had given her to understand that she was the chosen one. He couldn't inscribe her name because the matter was not official yet and he needed to formally propose.

She had a beautiful bust and profile. There was something Germanic in her appearance, since she did have a fair amount of German blood, but this was smoothed over by her Englishness.

He could not have chosen better. Only Louise might have made him hesitate, Louise d'Orléans, with her pretty little breasts. If only they hadn't been quite so small. Orléans women, since forever, were not well endowed, but they compensated for that lack by their wit. Wit counted. So did breasts.

But neither one nor the other counted as much as the hunt.

"Over there is the *ayuntamiento*, city hall. Say *ayuntamiento*."

"Ayun . . ."

"Ta . . ."

"Mento."

"Miento."

"Miento."

"To. Not *to-ooh. To.* Just *to."*

"To."

"Just like in French, which you speak so well. You are adorable!"

She was delightful. He was crazy about her.

Patricia was also fine, except a little big. He didn't like big women, even when they were attractive. And she, what did she think of him? Oh, what did that matter? Furthermore, when he dreamt about her, he pictured the face and figure of Maria Antonia von Mecklenburg-Schwerin. If he were a Sultan, he could have picked the two of them, or three or four!

"You're laughing. You haven't seen another parrot, have you?"

"No, my adorable one. One is enough."

Much clamor issued from around the square: the noise and confusion of the crowd, the blare of the band, the shouts, the horses' hooves on cobblestones. He had turned into the Calle del Sacramento. He would have to argue with the police, if it was barricaded at the top, and prove that he did, in fact, live where he said. "There, across the street at number 88. Please . . . Calle Mayor 88. Real Pensión. On the third floor at Mr. and Mrs. Rodríguez's." But how could he prove it?

The feeling of lightness persisted in spite of his great dismay. Each step launched him into the air, and he saw himself pass above the trees. Small groups of people ran so as not to arrive late: families with a grandmother bringing up the rear, shouting at them to wait for her, a child with a bloody knee who had fallen, his father patting it with a handkerchief.

It was a big day. A day like this hadn't occurred in a long time. Since when? Twenty-five years? Thirty years?

"No, Father, twenty-two."

"Really? Good. Anyway, it makes no difference."

"I remember," said a man leaning on a cane. "The procession went on the Calle Santiago."

"Santiago?" said the wife. "Are you certain, José? I seem to remember . . ."

"Absolutely certain," repeated the old man. "Because I say so! Santiago!"

"But in those days the Calle Santiago . . ."

"What? What about the Calle Santiago, then?" Irritated, the old man shook his cane.

"Good, but let's not stay here talking into thin air," said another woman, who could have been the first one's sister.

"Thin air, thin air . . . What's that supposed to mean?"

"That means we could botch this whole thing! The procession is moving forward, while we argue. Anyway, not Santiago, it's not possible!"

"What's not possible?"

"Not possible, no!"

She gesticulated, drew imaginary lines, tried to see how, even thirty years ago, one could arrive at the royal palace passing through the Calle Santiago. Her arm circled above people's heads. She still seemed unsure when another man, perhaps her husband, to settle the question stated precisely, "It was the king's wish."

"Maybe," she acknowledged. "But that still doesn't tell me how you could get to the palace passing through Santiago. Come, let's go."

Every morning for two months now, she had practiced pronouncing vowels very distinctly, not letting them drift into diphthongs, and also rolling her *r*'s. The *r*'s weren't too difficult because she had learned to roll them as a child in Scotland, hearing the gardeners and chambermaids at Balmoral. The vowels were another matter. Though basically, Spanish and French vowels weren't that different. It had taken Madame Mère three years without a teacher, using only an old manual, and being in contact with her sisters-in-law, to learn her new language. And she did it from German. *To. To. To.* To stop abruptly at the end. Keep the sound in check. Keep it from rising again and unraveling.

To. To. Ta. Te.

"Still a quarter of an hour, my beauty."

"Yes," she said. "We're arriving."

"66, 68. We're arriving. We're arriving. How wonderful! Our new life will begin as soon as we go through the gate."

"Yes."

With a pipi, she felt like adding. To begin with a pipi. Oh! My goodness! Pipiiiiiiiiii.

"But there, Officer, sir. There. Right there. There's a sign, do you see? Real. Real Pensión. It's big."

"I don't see a thing."

"But, yes! Vertical. Real Pensión. In red letters. I have the key here. Look at it."

"It doesn't prove anything. Everyone has a key in their pocket."

"With the name."

"That doesn't either, it doesn't . . ."

"One of your men could come with me."

"What makes you think that I can assign a man
to every passerby! And what are those flowers you're
holding? The king has forbidden the throwing of
flowers."

"It's not to throw them. They are a gift for someone. To celebrate an event."

"All right, go ahead. Be quick! The lead horses are
already here."

Fernando ran across the street and rushed upstairs.

There were people in the hall. The boarders were
clustered in front of the door to his room with Mr.
Rodríguez in the middle. They seemed to be waiting.

"Ah, Fernando. There you are! I wondered where
you could be. You left very early this morning."

"The same as usual," he said.

"Even today, yes. Listen. We need you. Your kind-
ness. This is what's happening . . ."

He had understood instantly. The boarders wanted
to see the procession go by from his balcony. The Rodríguez family was already on the other balcony, with
cousins who had come to Madrid especially, nephews,
friends, neighbors. And the other rooms had no balcony.

"I understand," he said.

"If you could just . . ."

"Just what?"

"Allow these gentlemen to . . ."

"Sorry, the answer is no."

"No?"

"No. I don't want anyone on my balcony."

"But . . . Fernando! You're all alone!"

"Maybe. But it's my room. I pay the rent and wish, in fact, to watch the procession all alone."

"You're joking!" said a young Galician, with whom he had gotten on quite well the night before.

"We'll pay you," said someone else.

"That's not the issue. Sorry, gentlemen, the answer is no. Don't insist."

"On a day like today," exclaimed Mr. Rodríguez.

"Because it's a day like today," he said, opening the door, which he quickly locked behind him.

From the beginning, outwardly cordial, the Rodríguezes had found him weird. They would take comfort now in that opinion. He had argued with a boarder over a bottle of wine: the boarder had accused him of taking it from an unoccupied table next to his, and the Rodríguezes had agreed with this maniac, when all they had to do was open another bottle without further fuss.

He went out on the balcony. Mrs. Rodríguez, from hers, made a reproachful gesture. On a day like today, when Spain should have been full of only merrymaking and brotherhood, joy and fellowship, a little generosity wouldn't have hurt, would it?

There was a window between the two balconies. The other "without-balcony" boarders squeezed around it. Their heads were like a large, moving cluster of grapes. He felt their eyes crawling on his back like leeches.

"It's forbidden to throw flowers," cried the young Galician.

"I know," he said without turning around.

The head of the procession appeared. One could hear the sound of both the iron-ringed wheels and the horses' hoofs. But now all one could see were the trumpeters and the heralds in their emblazoned capes. The first carriage was far behind. That of the young couple was even farther back; one could distinguish it only by the growing swell of the general uproar. Then, but perhaps it was an optical illusion, everything accelerated. Suddenly, the first three carriages were there, and the next three had already passed by the pretty salmon-pink Italian embassy. The horses, as if aware of the solemnity of the event, clacked their shoes. Unless, having been up since dawn, they thus showed their displeasure. Or they simply smelled the stable.

Three days earlier, Mrs. Rodríguez had seen him

throwing oranges and tomatoes into the street from his balcony.

"Fernando, what are you doing? You're crazy!"

"I'm amusing myself," he had answered.

"A strange way to amuse yourself! We'll have a visit from the police!"

"I adore the police."

"And what waste! Such beautiful tomatoes! I hope you didn't steal them!"

"Who do you take me for, Señora?"

She had looked him up and down and then said sullenly, "I don't know. I don't know what to think of you."

Since that incident, the Rodríguezes' distrust of him had greatly increased. Whenever they passed him —either one of them—they would cast a quick glance with looks filled with both reproach and fear. The desire to get rid of this troublesome fellow, as well as deprive him of a spectacle he seemed to await impatiently, visibly ran through their minds. He forced himself to be pleasant, fearing he might be thrown out before the big day.

Yesterday, he had planted himself in front of the landlady with a honeyed smile.

"There's no harm in loving your king, is there?" he'd said.

Troubled and dumbfounded, she'd asked herself what to make of this remark. Then her face had
cleared; with shining eyes she'd answered, "But of
course not, Fernando!"

She had even touched his arm. But now, once
again, from her overcrowded balcony, she stared at
him with hostility. What did it mean: him, alone, over
there, egotistical and solitary with his bouquet lying
on the railing . . . The rest of them crushed like sar-
dines. Only now it was too late. She could do nothing
about him.

What he loved most in life, besides hunting, were
parades. Those beautifully grand military machines
with their caparisons, plumes, ornamentations, ban-
ners, medals, and sabers. The bestoying of knight-
hood, trumpet blares, sounding the fall-in. The merry
jostling that took place when breaking rank. Everything sparkled, hullabalooed, whooped. Prussians
were champions in that department. Because of that
alone, he might have been partial to María Antonia.
Her thick neck and square shoulders were unfortunate . . . and the waist that presaged her mother's
stoutness . . . But that was all in the past. María Eugenia, his dear wife, his lovely new queen, still white
and intact sitting next to him, blonde as a dream born

of happiness, had with one simple stroke erased the image of all those faces that had, during the short course of his European peregrinations, trembled before his gaze. But she, María Eugenia, had something the others did not. Her seven rivals could possess a thousand qualities she lacked, but they would never possess hers: grace. María Luisa Gabriela of Savoy, the child queen, first wife of his ancestor, founder of the Spanish Bourbons, must also have had it. Philip V had been afraid that his future wife of less than thirteen was not yet nubile and sunk into the first of the four thousand six hundred and twenty-three melancholic crises that were to mark his existence. The meeting had taken place at the castle in Figueras. The boring nuptial dinner barely over, he had thrown himself upon her, like a beast, with all the blazing ardor of his eighteen years. Panic-stricken by this treatment, the little princess had barricaded herself in her room three nights running and swore the bloody game would never happen again, nor would she ever even sleep in the same bed as that gross lout. The lady-in-waiting, the Princess of Ursins, had to use all her artful powers of persuasion to make her understand that, on the one hand, it was her duty to please the king, her master, and, on the other, she would soon learn to enjoy what was less brutal than she imagined, not necessarily dirty, and which was often full of hidden sweetness. María Luisa took a liking to it even sooner than they had hoped. The royal couple spent the next five months in Barcelona, turbulent Catalan country, in endless *coitus ininterruptus.*

48

She could not be without her king, nor he without his queen. Not at all: not for an hour or even a minute. Alas, besides love, a king has his duties. From time to time, he must wage war. This king does battle but is always in a hurry to leave the field, to once again reunite with his dear wife; she, day and night, dreams only of him. Paradise would reign on earth, if she could always be united with him and he with her. No other war after that first one was ever able to separate them. She accompanies him to all of them and between fights they run off together, no matter where: the tottering castle of an unknown small nobleman spotted in the countryside, a convent full of terrified cloistered nuns, a barn, a woodcutter's hut, a flower-flooded field. They resume again the celebration of the singular marriage their existence has become.

Why did María Luisa, barely adolescent, have to die shortly thereafter? Those who had known her used the same word to describe her, one not often applied to children, and that was charm. She had charm as well as grace.

María Eugenia, too, had both. Suddenly, at number 84 of the Calle Mayor, the king of Spain's face darkened: charm, granted, and grace, but does she also have fire? María Eugenia Victoria of Battenberg, his queen, has she received from Providence that other gift as well, the essential gift, as indispensable to marriage as oxygen is to lungs? Without that flame his child wife possessed, that permanent flame, those inextinguishable coals where the great fire of our body draws its life force, Philip V would have died.

He clasps her arm very tightly. So tightly, she gives him an astonished look, forgetting the pipi.

"84, 86 . . . we've almost arrived," he says. "This time, we're really nearly there. Two hundred more meters, even less, a hundred and fifty."

"Yes," she says. "I already see 88, over there . . ."

"Yes, 88! Oh! My love, what joy!"

"Yes, my . . ."

She has pronounced his name. For the first time. Happy, yes, she will be happy with this man she still barely knows. Who jumps from one idea to the next with the gracefulness of a baby goat in a field.

She must tell him about the pipi. If not, seeing her burst out of the carriage like a madwoman, with her six-meter-long train that will tangle up with the horses' legs, he won't understand. He'll think that she has . . . God knows what!

"Listen . . ."

"Yes, my love."

"I must . . . Something . . . Leaving the church, I should have . . ."

"Say, darling, say!"

"You see, I . . ."

Years later, when the nightmares had stopped, when the gaudy scarlet of fresh blood had faded, when the screams had become muffled moans, only then did she think of a strange fact that should have puzzled her at that instant, even if it couldn't have changed anything: the fact that the bouquet from the balcony was falling too quickly.

In Biarritz, she had come in from the beach sooner than he to the lovely palace the French emperor had built, facing the ocean, for another Eugénie who was beautiful, strict, and severe. So full of mirrors, you spent most of the time running into your own likeness, or walking into a person coming from the opposite direction, who disappeared at the last second, kidnapped by another mirror, whom you found again later, stunted or ballooned, but always elusive. He

overtook her a few minutes later, or thought he had.
He ran from one corridor to another, leapt from one
mirror to the next, madly waving his arms, more and
more impatient to hold her against him. On the beach,
he had nuzzled his head in her neck, under her hair.
Now she felt his lips on her skin. For the first time;
deceptively secure in a small octagonal salon, open
on four sides, which crazily multiplied their double
pursuit of each other, she wondered just how far she
could push his ardor. She herself was less and less sure
of her capacity for resistance. She felt it dangerously
weakening. How to flee now, in this enchanted world
that delivered a thousand times over her perception of
a desired desire?

"Are you hurt? Darling! Darling! María! Answer me!
Are you hurt? Are you hurt?"

"No, I . . . I feel nothing . . ."

His tunic was torn. You could see his white shirt.
A piece of splintered wood struck his heart. Fortu-
nately, a medal deflected it. He would be dead without that medal.

"You see, medals are good for something!"

He makes a joke. He has the strength to joke amid
all the groans, the confusion and the blood, and the

thick and acrid smoke that won't dissipate. He shakes himself. He exults. He stands in the carriage and leans at the window to address the crowd.

"It's nothing!" he repeats. "Nothing. Nothing. We are not hurt. Neither the queen nor I. Everything is fine. Give me your hand, dearest, to show the Spanish people, our people, that we are uninjured. That the act of an imbecile, of a criminal, could not harm us."

Nevertheless, the Spanish people continue to shout that the king is dead and also the queen. What a tragedy! Such a beautiful couple!

Those cries—*dead! dead!*—will re-echo in her head from year to year, beyond the fracas of a great war, and then another great war, and many lesser but still terrible wars between those two, before and after, and during the course of a long life.

He helps her get out of the carriage. He has given orders to prepare the coach of "respect," which always follows the royal carriage in processions. Gestures have become slow. People move sluggishly in the midst of panic.

As she steps forward, she discovers that her dress is bloody, she herself is covered with blood, and her white satin slippers are black with it. There is blood everywhere: on the hangings of the carriage, on the curtains, on the windows, on the cobblestones; the coachman lies between the wheels, torn to pieces; the street is strewn with the bodies of horses, soldiers, and spectators. The blood drips and splashes. Even the sky is bespattered. A shower of blood has beaten down on Madrid. She flounders, as if in a swamp. It sticks to her hands, her legs, her neck. Her feet are like balls of hardened blood. She walks between bodies. One is headless. Blood bubbles in the hole of her neck, like in the painting that depicts the beheading of Anne Boleyn at either Balmoral or Kensington, kept hidden from visitors.

Another person is legless but smiles beneath his plumed military cap. She stumbles ahead, something catches her ankle, it's a rope, no, it's bowels, entrails of horses or men. When she collapses into the new carriage, she feels sticky and stinking, and thinks she was right not to eat anything this morning. Blood, her blood, beats in her temples, in her neck, as if demanding to be freed from the prison of her body to mix with all the blood that flows up and down the street, reaching the Puerta del Sol.

Someone holds her up, she doesn't know who. She walks. On the tiles. It's the courtyard. The courtyard of the palace. It is he, the king. His arm. Her king. He was very brave last year in Paris, when a bomb was thrown at the carriage where he sat next to the president of the Republic. "The hazards of the calling," he said laughingly.

She is in the palace, still wearing her dress stiff-ened with blood. She should remove it and wash, but she doesn't have the strength. Has anyone sent her mother and the king of England a telegram of reas-surance?

"Yes. Rest now, my darling. Your women will help you change. You must not leave that on. Look, it's hor-rible!"

It is horrible. She has taken off her stained shoes, blackened by the blood of some unknown person, but she needs time for the dress. She wants to simply breathe, try to make some sense out of the unbearable hubbub, the continual dazedness in her head. She does not want to be touched.

"Lie down, my darling. We have time. Everything has to be reviewed and reorganized."

Everything, that's right.

"In any case. I don't want a ball. We have already danced enough!"

Always joking. She would like to laugh but doesn't have the strength. She is empty. Her skin consists of nothing anymore.

". . . in an hour."

What's in an hour? Her heart beats against her ribs. She is a bird in a cage, a piece of living, torn, liv-ing, flesh is all she is.

"The meal, darling," the king continues, her king. "We have to eat, don't we?"

To eat. She hasn't eaten since last night, but she isn't hungry. Her throat is in knots. Knotted, closed, dry, forever. She still smells blood. That's what's hardest of all. Foul smell. Slithering deep down inside her, like an unending snake.

"To eat?"

"Yes, my darling, eat! Better that we all eat together, rather than alone, don't you think? I'm sure you're hungry. Aren't you? María! Speak to me!"

"Yes . . ."

She doesn't know if she's hungry. Knows nothing.

Her king goes on talking. He talks and smiles. She watches his lips and his teeth and his pink tongue, all the way back. His lips continue moving through the ferocious din of the bomb that keeps on exploding in her head.

There he is! There he is! Hold him! He waits for the shout, or shouts, but it's quiet. On the staircase, he had elbowed the Galician, heard his body tumble down the stairs, and now he runs. Heads swivel. The eyes of Madrid gaze hungrily at his back. The footsteps of Madrid hammer the ground behind him. The footsteps of justice on the march. His head is a furnace. His lungs are burning bellows. He stops.

Idiot. Of course, the train station is the first place they'll expect him. Waiting to pick him like a flower.

To hide. But where in a city where the trees themselves are suspect? He starts running again, but in the opposite direction, with the rescue teams and the ambulances. He daringly mingles with them, helping transport stretchers, supporting the staggering and bloodied wounded. Farther along the street, he breaks away, overcome by the intrusive odor of blood, takes an unknown street, and finds himself in front of the columns of the Royal Theater. There, a crazy idea hits him. Yes! Why not! He has nothing more to lose. And it's the last place they would ever think of to look for him.

Ambassadors, princes, dukes stand in line to congratulate him. He behaved admirably. A hero from the past: one worthy of the Spanish tradition of gallantry and contempt for death. And how wonderful that he should be unhurt! The queen, too, his delightful, radiant wife.

"Already last year, sire, God wanted . . ."

"Yes, last year! As a matter of fact, today is precisely the anniversary. It's been a year, a year to the day. An attempted assassination a year . . . That, too, that will become a tradition, ha, ha, ha! Last year, a small bomb . . ."

"This year a big one, sire!"

"It's the same one! It grew larger."

With a king such as this, they all think, Spain is in good hands.

Indeed, the bomb has grown larger. The first tallies begin to arrive. Twenty dead have already been counted, especially in the retinue, and at least fifty wounded. Among the invited, some wished the ball would take place in spite of everything, if only to show the anarchists that royalty will not be intimidated by their pitiful fantasies. But the Prince of Wales and the Queen Mother are opposed to the idea. However, the decision is up to the king and he has already decided: wedding banquet, yes, ball, no. He says the queen insists that the banquet be held as planned. It would be an insult to the Spanish people, who love their kings and queens, to cancel everything. The Spanish people have only just begun to hear the news.

The queen is resting for the time being. She was magnificent. She didn't break down for an instant, as he helped her to cross the sea of blood. The most dreadful aspect of the horror, besides the sight of the wounded and the dead, is the smell. That repulsive mixture of sweet and sour, honeyed bitterness, that penetrates everywhere. You smell it in your nose, in your lungs, on your tongue. It has followed the procession like an evil vermin, climbed over the gates, and glided into the heart of the palace. To escape from it, the guests move back to open the windows with jerky movements, only to realize immediately it has come in from there, too.

The king circulates among the groups, patting arms and shoulders, kissing hands.

"Come now, it's over," he says to a German princess, collapsed on a chair. "We won't think about it anymore. Life is beautiful, Spain is great. Prussia, Bavaria, and England are great. Tomorrow we'll go duck hunting, and kings are eternal."

"They are part of the natural order of things," someone says behind him.

It's a Grand Duke of Russia, he doesn't know which one, there are so many, endowed with a bushy mustache and droopy eyelids.

"You are right, my good man," he says.

"It's so obvious," confirms a French duchess of Bourbon blood, although he is ignorant of how much or from which side.

And then they all burst out laughing simultaneously. Their laughter redoubles, because that, too, the act of laughing before and after danger, is, like the hunt, in the natural makeup of kings.

———

She has washed, powdered, and perfumed herself. Her ears were buzzing but now the drone is feebler and only a soft whistling sound persists. Her eyes are still slightly red from the residue of smoke hanging in the air. Sensitive eyes are a family trademark passed down from one generation to the next. No one will notice at dinner.

A shadow approaches, stops. It is he. He sits next to her on the sofa.

He kisses her, with ardor, on the cheek. She does not stir.

"Are there deaths?"

"I don't know," he answers. "Yes, I believe there are. So it seems. Inevitably. There are always victims in this kind of affair."

"Many?"

"Yes, many. Maybe. Darling, don't think about it anymore. The police and the army are working on it and know what has to be done. They have their schedules and lists. They will catch the guilty person and hang him like the dog he is. Royalty is safe; we have been through this before."

"It's horrible," she says. "Have the telegrams been sent?"

"Yes, yes, to everyone. Don't be uneasy, darling. Your mother has already responded."

"What does she say?"

"She thanks God."

"And Mother? Yours?"

"Well, you've seen her. She was here a while ago. She is resting but will be at the dinner. I'll fetch you in twenty minutes, so rest until then." He leaves.

The sun carves out a golden trapezoid on the rug. Violet looks red, yellow green.

She stands up to go to the window but is as if nailed on the spot. She cries out. As if someone, hidden under the sofa, had reached out to grab her ankle. But there is nothing, no one. She tries another step. And now, it's as though . . . it's like earlier, in the street, getting out of the carriage. The foot doesn't come forward. Everything else moves but not the foot. One would think it was rebelling, reclaiming its autonomy. She has to pull very hard. Even then, the foot barely moves. It's an invisible cord. Like the smell, it has followed her and holds her back, like a lasso.

"They must mistake him for a laborer. He has never seen such long corridors. Huge paintings of dead kings imprisoned in gaudy golden frames line the corridors. People pass him, talking excitedly. A meteorite has fallen in the sea, and the waves never stop spreading.

Then someone stares at him. A woman. A du-
enna. He must be cautious and appear to be entrusted
with an urgent duty.

The king is unhurt. Unhurt, unhurt. He went by
three women repeating the word. Five minutes ago,
his hope had swelled again. One woman lying pros-
trate on a velvet-covered bench was crying her heart
out. It had to have been for another reason. With all
those dead, there was much to cry about, although
people have cried for thousands of years.

Botched. It is botched. He has no further doubt.
A door will open, and the king of Spain whom he
wanted, was to have, killed will walk through it
fresh as a daisy. Ferrer is surely not happy. To have
planned the deed so brilliantly, only to see it fail at
the last minute. "They must tumble. All those crowns,
all those heads! After this, Romania, Bulgaria, Italy.
And finally, Germany, Russia, and England!" Ferrer is easily carried away by his dreams. But without
dreams, how do you reach your goal? How do you
live? Every ideal holds many dreams within. The
crazier they are, the better for the effectiveness of the
movement.

No one knows him in Madrid. Aside from his false
name, the Rodríguezes are ignorant of anything else
about him. To them, he is only the Fernando Matorral of his fake identity card. Madrid is big. He'll live

elsewhere, grow a mustache, and start again in six months. Kings must die.

A group is coming in his direction. Suddenly, he realizes what he must really look like, not a workman but a dust-covered tramp. How did they ever allow him into the church? To prove that a royal wedding is also a popular festival? That all classes of society have the right to be represented? Not now, not in five minutes, but he'll be arrested for sure. Fernando Velasco-Matorral has exhausted his share of luck. Failure will then be complete. He could have armed himself, but Ferrer was against the idea: too risky. As a result, he has nothing but his stiletto. He takes three steps back and manages to slip between a pair of tapestries. His mud-spattered shoes show under their hem. He wipes them off with his handkerchief and, risking everything to win it all, comes out of his hiding place, head down, resolutely advancing as though he were on a special mission. The approaching group—four men, two in uniform—does the same. They also are called on an urgent mission. They reach him, pass on by, and continue at the same pace.

Saved! His heart beats violently. Saved, but a prisoner. If he was able to enter the palace without difficulty, blending into the mob of guards and policemen and taking advantage of the general confusion, how will he manage to leave? Blinded by his boldness, he hasn't thought of that. His real name may be unknown to everyone, but not to the police. Those who know a man named Velasco, in Barcelona and elsewhere, those who were close to him and saw him frequently, are done for. Ferrer is better known than anyone. The palace is entirely surrounded by a high barrier, each pole topped by a large gold arrow. Over the past few days, he has studied the sites but has forgotten to count the number of openings and sentry boxes. How negligent!

He has entered a small salon whose stale smell tells him it is never used. He can stay there, but for how long and for what?

He has not killed the king. He has not accomplished his mission. He has acted unwisely and rashly. In truth, only one mistake but an enormous one: impatient, he dropped the bomb a few seconds too soon. He could see the royal carriage, the next-to-last one in the procession. He knew because of its size and its gold ornamentation. Why then did he aim for the preceding one? In order not to kill the king? To spare the queen?

He has killed innocent people. "There will always be victims, innocent and otherwise. As many as we kill, the number will always be less than the number our enemies kill every day to maintain their system of oppression." The reasoning is flawless. He has thought about it deeply and turned it over every which way in his mind. There is also another element in the mix: he, Fernando Matorral, likes a job that is clean and tidy and well executed. He is the last member of a line of leather craftsmen. Only his father, like a mole shut inside his mine, worked at a task lacking in dignity.

He has left the small salon where he has no business being. He must find a way into the gardens. An idea comes to him. One more.

"My love, you must. You must."

"I haven't the strength . . ."

"It's your first duty as queen. You cannot steal away. Not from this."

"If I had the strength, I . . ."

"Later, you may rest. Until evening."

She is white as a sheet. All the blood has flowed inside of her. Her lifeless hand, both too light and too heavy, rests on the balustrade. He brings it to his lips.

The word "evening" renewed his stiffness. His rod, an erect mast in the middle of his body, is ebony, steel. What will he do if nothing changes? What if, stubbornly, it has decided to keep this sign of hardness until the consummation?

"I leave you now, María Eugenia, and shall return

in ten minutes. I will give the order to delay the first course a quarter of an hour."

He exits, climbs the staircase, and reaches his private quarters. He feels, around the erect baobab of his pubis, an intense, painful tingling. What will happen this evening if she has not recovered, if she wants to see a doctor or has a fever? What if she goes to sleep and doesn't wake up until morning, then what will he do? Watch over her, as taut as a bow with an arrow ready to fly?

Someone knocks. It must be Mother. It is Mother.

The Queen Mother announces: "The duke is dead."

The duke? What duke? He doesn't know or care. He explodes with happiness amid the dust and the blood; he has the prettiest wife in the world and this wife, already his in the eyes of God, soon will be his in the flesh.

"Something opened up his belly."

"Who? Ah! Yes, that duke."

"A piece of metal, perhaps from the bomb."

"Yes, but you, Mother, are alive!"

He embraces her. He rarely embraces his mother. The Habsburgs rarely embrace. After so many years, he still hasn't lost hope of "Bourbonizing" her.

"I liked him very much," she says.

"Who? Oh! Yes."

"It's a disaster."

"Yes," he replies vaguely.

"Nevertheless, we're doing everything we can, aren't we?"

Everything? Everything what? What does she mean? And, who? We? And for whom? The Spanish people, probably. Kings "do" everything and, in return for their sacrifice, people want to kill them. It's unjust. It's unjust but it can't be helped. We will never prevent the sick fringes of society from committing horrible acts.

"And María Eugenia?"

"She is resting, Mother. In fifteen minutes, it all will be erased."

"What do you mean?"

"She will be completely recovered. You must understand, she has been very upset."

"I do understand. I, too, have been upset."

"There is reproach in those words. Never mind."

The tingling continues, getting worse. The ants are getting bigger. Even so, on a day like today he can't indulge in an adolescent's vice. If he had the time, he would jump on the first horse he could and gallop off. This calms him the best, riding all out, across the countryside. The Bourbons have always lived on a horse.

The door opens.

"Sire, we only await Your Majesties."

"What? What? Everyone is seated but us? Come, Mother, the soup will get cold."

Madame Mère purses her lips: the soup! What language! My God, her son is incorrigible.

She concentrates on breathing deeply. She hasn't vomited, in spite of that ghastly sugary taste in her mouth. Sweet and bitter. She hasn't eaten since yesterday, but gastric juices rising up from her stomach are in the mix.

The table is L-shaped. A single long table, with the royal couple seated in the middle, would have been better. But it's all the same to her. The immediate business at hand is the soup, which she must swallow and keep down. If she manages to, it will be victory number one. Other struggles, many others, lie in wait before the cock crows. This is her big day. Spain is watching her. And England, too, even though she doesn't belong there anymore.

Facing her is Pilar, Princess Pilar, who is she anyway? The king's sister? Another sister-in-law? A cousin? Whose? She'll find out. So many things to learn. Her life was simple and sweet, and now, suddenly, everything has become incredibly complicated.

She doesn't understand a word of what people are saying, as soon as they stop speaking French. So few of them speak French well. As for English . . . Those who, out of politeness, risk it have such thick accents that she wavers between trying to concentrate and bursting out laughing.

One thing, then another. Soup first. Half a spoonful. She feels the liquid hot and thick go straight down her pipe, which reminds her of that other one, bestowed upon women by God for the preservation of mankind. Pipes everywhere: up, down, front, back. How she wishes she could talk about this to someone. But how? They'd think she was crazy. Impossible. Simply impossible. No one would understand, even those who are most insightful and sensitive. No one. She can't discuss these things with anyone: not Mummy, not Madame Mère. These things in command of her body, whose existence must remain secret. Between her and herself.

Something is happening around Pilar. On her left, Pilar has a Chinaman, on her right, an Arab. The Chinaman has stood up. What's the matter with him? A stomachache? No. He has taken the place-card with his name written on it. To do what? He goes from one guest to another, comparing his to theirs, circling the table. Everyone is watching. Then he sits down again. The guests exchange smiles: it's a way to forget the drama playing out inside each one. Pilar tries to speak to the Chinaman, in the two or three languages she knows. None of these include Chinese, or Arabic, apparently the only language her other neighbor speaks. A system of gestures has been established between the three of them that gains the attention of the assembled guests and brings new smiles to their lips. Suddenly, one of those unexplainable funny little accidents happens, perhaps because of the bustle and stir. Princess Pilar's brooch falls, plop, into her plate. New smiles, this time dissimulated and hidden, because they risk becoming outright laughter. However, it's not over. Without waiting for the arrival of the butler, the Arab prince, to be helpful, dips his fingers in the soup bowl and fishes out the jewel. After which, even more considerately, perhaps by virtue of some native custom, he wipes it with the tablecloth and then—yes, yes!—puts it in his mouth. He sucks it like a candy, displays it on his tongue, takes it and wipes it anew, this time with his napkin, and finally offers the brooch to the poor princess, whose eyes are appealing wildly all around for help. Gathering up her courage, blushing all over, she resolves to take it but not refasten it at the neck, which now looks nakedly bare.

If, by chance, one of the guests should venture to relate the tale, the story of the incident might easily spread abroad and, someday, find itself in a history book: a burlesque conclusion to the "tragedy" of that day.

After the soup, a flaky pastry that appears a bit greasy; when she turns it over, more than greasy, it is saturated in fat. Spanish cooking is overly heavy and fatty for her taste. Will she ever manage to like it? Madame Mère, who has lived longer in Spain than in Austria, is still not used to the food. For twenty-five years, she has nibbled and picked at her food. So her daughter-in-law will follow suit and nibble and pick. She eats half the pastry with tremendous effort, and then falls upon the cucumber slices accompanying it.

"Isn't it good, my darling? Don't you like it?"

"It's slightly heavy."

"The pastry? Really? And I can't stand cucumbers. What a pair we make! They might have consulted us! I should scold the person responsible. But no, too bad. I have better things to do today! Ha! Ha!"

Everything makes him laugh, her king. He loves to laugh. How lucky. At seventeen, dreaming of her future, she saw herself married to a boring, fat duke. Instead of the duke, she has a king who is neither fat nor boring. Will she be lucky in her life? Was she born under a good star? A poor orphan who becomes a queen . . . That's what a fortune-teller told her in either Perigueux or Poitiers—some gray city en route to Biarritz. One afternoon when her mother was tired, she had escaped Miss Dorritt's eye and found herself in a smelly passageway, at the end of which was a rickety staircase; at the very top, in a room full of rugs and copper pots, sat a gypsy with huge earrings, just like in pictures. Poor Mummy! If she had only known! "A long and happy life . . . Yes . . . Yes . . . But at the beginning, difficult. Yes, difficult. I see blood . . . Yes, yes . . . Blood . . . Lots of blood . . . But afterward, dawn breaks . . . The dawn of a great destiny . . ."

A great destiny. She, who only wishes for a tiny bit of one . . .

"Try this. You should like it very much, my pretty queen. I'm not sure what it is, but it looks delicious."

They have set a new plate in front of her: on the plate is a dark blob that looks like an organ. It's not a liver or a large kidney or something from a bull (they wouldn't dare). A piece of mystery drowning in a shiny, runny black sauce that stains the china. She gazes, fascinated, at the unknown object, which once lived, unable to persuade herself that it must enter her and, once inside, become part of her flesh. Absorbed in her disgust, she forgets to give back the three ounces of soup she managed to swallow.

Thanks to him, it's as though the palace already belonged to the people: doors wide open, passages breached, freed for a few hours from its customary interdictions. It's all his accomplishment. If Ferrer knew, would he forgive the failure of the operation? When the end result miscarries, Ferrer is indifferent to details as well as symbols. But we'll discuss that later, Don Fernando, between you and yourself. For now, it's a question of following the garden paths. They are beautiful, straight paths, bordered by boxwood hedges, culminating in elegant arabesques farther along. There a man rakes the gravel as though nothing had happened. From time to time he bends down to pick a weed. It shouldn't be too difficult. He has practiced on a man made of straw; straw may not be flesh but he knows where to strike: the safest place being the nape of the neck between the vertebrae. That's the location for the screw to penetrate during the *garrota vil* torture, the punishment awaiting anarchists, nihilists, and all the king's enemies. For you, also, Fernando, if you miss the mark. Later, if you succeed.

He begins to follow the long hedge along its length, nonchalantly at first, then faster and bowing down, so as not to be seen too soon by his victim.

Dear Mummy,
Just a word, right away, to reassure you. I want to confirm what you must have already been

told in the telegrams: everything is fine. I wasn't
hurt, and neither was he. As you can imagine,
it was horrible at the time. But now, everyone
has recovered, and he, my darling king, has
been marvelous. You should have seen him:
not an instant of panic or nervousness. His feet
wading in blood, he had only one concern: to
calm, to reassure, and to allay the fear in everyone. He joked, laughed. These Spaniards
are extraordinary. I've never seen a more coura-
geous people; all the others, too, including the
Queen Mother, my dear mother-in-law. Imagine, dear Mummy, there were three deaths in
her carriage, which preceded ours. But she and
her two daughters, my sisters-in-law, nothing!
How can I thank you, God Almighty?

The ball has been canceled, which is a good
thing. I honestly don't think anyone felt like
dancing. I couldn't have, and he didn't particularly care. I don't think he really likes to
dance. The dinner, on the other hand, was held
as planned. As my dear king said, after all, we
must eat. In any case, everything was so greasy;
I could hardly swallow a bite. But, rest assured,
I feel fine. I'll recover tomorrow with a good
British sandwich!

A Spanish princess, whom I still can't quite

73

place, sat opposite me. She may be another one of my sisters-in-law. The poor woman was flanked by a Chinese (or Japanese) gentleman and an Arab, I imagine, wearing a white robe and one of those funny headdresses they have, you know. She tried to talk to them but they didn't understand a word. And then, as if that weren't enough, she dropped her brooch in the bowl. Yes, in her soup, poor soul! You should have seen it! But wait, that's not all. Her Arab neighbor turned it into a wonderful occasion to demonstrate his gallantry. He simply plunged his hand in the soup, retrieved the jewel, put it in his mouth . . . yes, his mouth . . . licked it with his tongue, and returned it, with an elegant gesture, to its owner! Said owner having no idea where to hide! And me neither!

The only advantage of this incident was that it provided a distraction from the other. What a horrendous thing that was! All that blood! I still see it all around me like a sea! And, more especially, I smell it!

This is the big night, dear Mummy, when I shall become both queen and wife. I so wish you were next to me, dear Mother, yes, next to me. I say what I feel. At least, in the next room. You must think that's absurd and ridiculous, but it's the truth. I'm so afraid of being clumsy. I know you've told me I have nothing to do in all of this except to yield, to give myself over, to be led, that's all. But . . . really nothing? Still, I have my doubts. Anyway, tomorrow will be better. It will be over. For now, I need air.

"This is ridiculous! Ridiculous! The last time I saw her, she was sitting right there at her desk, writing a letter! A while ago! Twenty minutes! And no one saw her leave? That's impossible!"

He repeats "That's impossible" three times and storms out into the hall. His footsteps diminish and all of a sudden grow louder again.

"Good! Pedro! Come here! I want a methodical search. Not a lot of people looking every which way to give the impression they're doing something!"

He's very angry. Tonight of all nights!

He gave orders to the servants, the housekeepers, the doctors, his aide-de-camp not to let her out of their sight for one minute. And the result: gone, flown away, evaporated!

"Her Majesty, herself, Sire . . ."

"Fine. If she wished it, withdraw, but no farther than three feet! Watch her! She is very emotional about this whole affair, as are we all. But the queen, even more so. She arrives in Spain, her new country, and minutes later everything blows up. What a welcome! You must be vigilant! If necessary, hide behind the curtains!"

They search for her on every floor of the south wing. No point looking in the north wing. She can't be there or in the gardens. Her shoes are still in the boudoir. What did she leave in? Slippers? Bare feet? The whole thing is crazy! Oh! My God! Provided that . . . She had wanted to walk a few steps and . . . She has fallen! She is stretched out somewhere, unconscious, very near here, in an alcove! In this place that is full of nooks and crannies, small hidden staircases . . .

For the first time, he's terrified. God is punishing him. Who is testing his love and why? What could be stronger than his love for his queen? He has proven it. He will prove it to her even more! And the bloody dress is still there! Didn't anyone think to remove it? What are they all doing here with their arms dangling?

"No one dares touch it, Sire. It is sacred."

"Yes, sacred. Fine, as you wish. It still must be put elsewhere. We can't leave it here forever!"

He collapses onto a chair. To wait: what he hates most. But what else can he do? And wait for what?

He leaps to his feet.

"Go away! Clear out of here! All of you! Surely you realize you won't find her in this room."

He had grabbed it under the arms. A dead body weighs twice as much as a living one. He had dragged it along the path. The feet traced two straight lines in the mud, like those of the other dead man, now in the gravel at the end of the path.

Damasio was his favorite uncle. The police had left the body on the spot after the riot to set an example. It was still warm, like this one, two hours later. As a child, he used to accompany him hunting. It was Damasio who had taught him to shoot. Ah! Those delicious moments, when they lay side by side on the dewy grass. Catalan hares were more cunning than their naïve Castilian cousins, and they ran faster as well. You needed lots of patience and guile to bring back more than two in your game bag. Blasted by a buckshot, they whirled in the air before tumbling down and dying. What a sense of elation, then, to dig your fingers into their reddened fur and to feel their inert little corpses that seem to still palpitate.

Returning home one day, he wondered if a gun couldn't kill something besides hares. He was twelve years old. What did Uncle Damasio think? He didn't talk much and expressed himself badly, but he did understand how society functioned; society was irredeemable and needed to be destroyed.

He throws the body into a thicket, at the end of the path, and attempts to remove its smock. He has clumsily fastened the clasps instead of opening them. While trying to do so, he thinks about other poor souls, like this one, who must die before cries of victory are heard.

He was seven. It was at Aranjuez, his favorite palace, built by his favorite ancestor, Philip V, who, in spite of his congenital illness, had done so much for Spain. Fighting your enemies was nothing. The real enemy was himself, whom he had had to confront every minute of his life. Seven years old. He had hidden in a clump of begonias. They were looking for him everywhere. Two feet away, men were having lively discussions. Officers. He could have touched their boots with his little hand. It was so much fun. Mother was crying. The tutor was crying. Officers, footmen, everyone was crying, running, searching. In the meantime, there he was, right there, invisible. Invisible, immobile, and all-powerful. Turned to stone with joy. He was Philip V, who held the whole empire—from Mexico to the

Philippines, from the Marianne Islands to Tierra del Fuego—in the palm of his hand.

"Asleep? At this hour? But where? Where?"

"Majesty . . ."

"Look in the orange grove also. You never know. Or look again in the palace."

"We have searched everywhere in the palace, Majesty."

"Everywhere!" cried Mother. "Don't talk nonsense, Teodoro! The palace is not a tool shed! You say you've searched everywhere?"

"Yes, Majesty."

"Very well. You may begin again!"

He remembers the river. Father had gone downstream to see if they were biting better there. Fish had their habits, which varied with the seasons. He had caught only two since this morning. Mother would want at least a dozen to cook up a good dish. She was waiting at home, frying pan at the ready.

The sun was playing on the surface of the water. It was spreading big gobs of gold that changed shape endlessly. Because the day was hot and the birds were trilling, he climbed to the top of the slope. He saw Father all the way down there where the fish were biting better. He had a silvery one wriggling on the end of his line, skimming the water. A beautiful sight. The world was beautiful. He didn't know then that this magnificent world was also cruel and, most especially, unjust. One must never stop being innocent. He really should have died in childhood. At seven years of age. Before the first revelation.

Ferrer would not be pleased if he could hear him now.

Father put down his fishing rod. He climbed back slowly along the riverbank. He called out and looked all around. He drew near the water, brushed aside the reeds, went on tiptoe to see farther, called out again with his head thrown back. He was afraid. His son didn't know how to swim yet. He might have slipped. The child, as if in a trance of happiness, was up there watching him. He had gone down the slope again but, rather than joining his father directly in order to dispel his fears, decided to play a trick on him and had hidden behind a boulder. Father continued to call out his name. He had let him call a long time, too long, perhaps. He regretted it to this day. Later, when he did rejoin him with a cry of joy, encircling his legs with his arms, his father had pushed him away without a hug and then had hit him a long time, until his rage was spent. He had not forgotten that, either. Was his father responsible for this condition? Soon after, he died in the depths of his mine.

Happiness is an accident. It can strike no matter where, even at the heart of anguish: like now. He has had many such miraculous moments during his short life. So many. But this one surpasses whatever he could have imagined. The possibilities are endless now for anything to happen. The cruelest of deaths can never hollow him out completely. A sudden conviction dazzles him: he knows he will die, but whichever way he dies, he will die happy.

They search for her everywhere—what madness on her part. Like at Warrington Grounds, at the Duke of Westminster's, when she was nine. With Mary—the other Mary—Judith, and Charles, she had climbed up to the roof of the big tower. They had gone down, but she hadn't followed them, she had stayed up there, just because, out of pure pleasure. For the pleasure of knowing they would look for her, which indeed they did. She heard their voices, their footsteps, doors opening and closing, the scraping of ladders. It was delicious. She shivered, at that moment, out of sheer innocence. It was different now, but not so different. People walked directly by the beam, behind which she was lying in thick dust. Mother had been crazy with anguish: it was just after Father's death. Finally she had reappeared for Mummy's sake. She had told a huge lie, her one and only, simply because the truth was impossible to articulate. After that, she never lied again. "I went to sleep." Her mother's tears turned to tears of joy. "Asleep! Fell asleep! My little darling fell asleep!" What could she say this time, not to her mother but to her king?

The man has a big, strong chest, covered with thick black hair. Her fingers run through it. They stick a little because he is sweaty. And he? Her king? Is he hairy? Perhaps not. Or only three or four, in the middle. Aristocrats are bald. Oh! My God! Things that . . . Has she the right to think such things about her love? Dense black hair is nice. It's beautiful. It's pleasant to caress. She never would have imagined it could be so peaceful.

Abruptly, in a single second of violent foreshortening, María Eugenia, queen of Spain, understands two essential things. The first is that if she is found here, naked with a half-naked gardener in his shed, not only is she lost, but the scandal will be so great that war might even break out between England and Spain. The second is that this gardener is not a gardener. She sees the fast-falling flowers and, at the very top, between the flowers, on the edge of a balcony, a

fierce face ablaze. The same face she is caressing at
this very moment, the face of the man who hurled the
flowers, the assassin who annihilated dozens of lives
and made a woman out of her.

Loud voices outside draw near. Among the ten
words of Spanish she knows is the word "stay."

"*Quedar . . . quedas . . . quedat . . . aquí.*"

"*Sí,*" he says.

"*Esperas.*"

"*Sí.*"

Listening to the voices, she dresses in the dark and
leaves. She runs along the freshly raked gravel. Someone over there has seen her and turns around. There is
shouting and assembling of groups. One shape stands
out clearly: it is he. He runs faster than the others.

"My darling! María Eugenia! My love!"

She must explain. She has so much to say, but she
can only mime the words that at present she needs to
rest. They bring a sedan chair that hasn't been used
in over a century. She is transported in this ridiculous
box, with the king walking beside her, to a room on
the ground floor where she is left alone with him.
He kisses her all over, presses her against him, and
touches her breasts for the first time. She signals to
him: no, not yet. She needs tranquility now of both
mind and spirit.

"I went outside for a breath of air and . . ."

"For a breath of air? Where? Tell me! Tell me!"

"For . . . I don't . . ."

"What happened?"

"Then . . ."

"Then what? What?"

"I . . . I don't know anymore . . . I . . . I'm so sorry . . . I'm very sorry . . ."

"What? What are you sorry about?"

"The trouble that . . . that I've caused you . . ."

"You can tell me later. María! Oh! I was so terribly alarmed, my love! Terribly! We didn't know where to look anymore! I was desperate."

"I . . . I should have . . . I don't know . . . got lost . . ."

"Yes! It's the aftershock. It's normal. But you are here, my darling, you are here. That is what . . . The rest is nothing! Nothing at all! But do you know what?"

"I don't know anything . . . tell me . . . my dear . . ."

He then tells her they have found a body at the bottom of the garden. They don't know yet who it is. Well, yes, they do know: no one. It is no one. A gardener. Or a footman. At first, they thought it was one of the victims of the attempted assassination who had come there to die. But why there? And how? Some unknown person who, half-conscious, might have walked from the Calle Mayor to the bottom of the garden, crossing the palace courtyard and then the palace itself, in all of its breadth. But how would he have entered the palace? That's when they discovered the wounds from a steel dagger on the body. Three blows, a deep one at the nape of the neck.

Therefore, it must be something else, unrelated to the crime. In any case, they don't know. They make assumptions, the most unlikely among them being the most plausible. They even ask themselves if it couldn't be the perpetrator of the crime himself. Distraught at not accomplishing his goal, he might have entered the palace and the gardens to complete his mission. But entered how? How? They still had no answer. Or, disappointed once again, he would not have been able to endure his failure and so committed suicide. Or, taken by surprise, might have killed the troublesome witness. Or killed the gardener to take his clothes. In fact, the dead man was half-naked. But his clothes . . . Ah! How many riddles! The investigation may shed light on these mysteries, and it has only just begun.

María Luisa's death caused a profound and limitless sorrow in Philip V. His predisposition to melancholy developed overnight, but there was also a physiological problem. Philip V, inconsolable widower, could remain inconsolable but not a widower. Abstention was, for him, unbearable. Mistresses were suggested as a solution, but he didn't like the idea. He wanted a wife: recognized, legitimate, and permanent. The search began for a marriageable princess. Spanish ambassadors at the courts of Europe were bidden to root one out and suspend all other business. Finally, after many negotiations and intrigues, this pearl was found at the court of Parma. Isabelle Farnese was fat, ugly, pockmarked, inconsequential, and disagreeable. Her greatest occupation was to stuff herself with cheese and butter. This overeating masked great ambition. The enfeebled and sickly king would be a convenient stepping stone toward what, besides getting even fatter, she most aspired to: power.

Did she love her husband? Was it pure ambition that enabled her to put up with his manias, his filthiness, his insatiable appetite? In fact, he died in her arms after thirty-one years of a wonderful marriage in every way. Every way. He can't be separated from her for one moment during a third of a century. They do everything together. They go to bed and get up together. They pray and hear mass every day together, they play billiards and piquet together, they eat together, read pious books together, receive the court together, stroll together, and ride together. When one of them is sick, the other does not leave the bed. They

trade their illnesses and, when she gives birth, he lies
next to her.

Madame Mère had had all the books that con-
tained intimate or scandalous stories banned from
all the palaces. This only incited the young king to
seek them out. Occasionally, he encountered a term
he didn't know the meaning of, but behind which he
sensed a troubling reality. So, it appeared his ancestor suffered from priapism. The accessible dictionaries
passed over the word, which only proved its licentious
definition.

And now, at eleven thirty, soon to be midnight, he
asks himself in anguish, sitting in his queen's (but not
yet his wife's) antechamber as she is sleeping still, if
he does not suffer from the same malady. His condition has already lasted twelve hours and the ten-
sion is so painful he wants to scream. Howling like
Philip V used to when, exceptionally, Isabelle arrived
late in coming to him.

A quarter of an hour after midnight. He has returned.
Her king, her beloved. He hesitated from entering the
room because he thought she was still too upset. How
considerate! How kind! Madly impatient, her beautiful king begins to undress. The clothes fly in the air,

drop on the rug: unnecessary finery. He himself has lit the candles placed in all four corners of the room. It must be a habit, a rite. The first night should take place in soft light just like this. The Bourbons are so romantic! So much more than the Saxe-Coburgs! Not to mention the Romanoffs.

Now she should close her eyes, give herself up absolutely and be engulfed in her offering. Immobile on her bed, she has already practiced in England: relaxed, yielding, surrendering. Suddenly, something . . . a force . . . there was no other way to describe it . . . a force, an unknown power . . . incomprehensible, impelled her to rise.

"What are you doing?" he asks, his voice altered with excitement.

"Stay like this, darling. Here. Don't move. I'll be back right away."

"Soon?"

"In a few minutes."

He must imagine her taking some personal precaution. A duty, perhaps. He's correct. It is a duty, intimate in some way. Imperative. Absolute.

She leaves. In bathrobe and slippers, she runs to the little staircase she had spotted two hours earlier, coming in from the garden. She goes down and opens the door. The garden is like a dark ocean, but she doesn't need to see in order to manage. Also, glimmers of light shine down from the topmost windows and play among the trees with more distant reflections. She runs, reaches the shed. She pays no attention to the utter darkness inside: he is there. She hears his breath rising from the bed of grasses. He sleeps. She smells the potent odor of his body.

"*Mi amor . . .* "

"*Mi amor,*" she whispers.

He wants to draw her to him, lightly touching her leg, and tries to hold her. She moves back. Like lightning, wordlessly—unless it be one of the ten words she had learned, *pureza*—she pulls out from a chink in the wall the stiletto he had killed the gardener with, which she had hidden before leaving the shed. With dispassionate and expert moves, disguised as caresses, she locates on his chest the two ribs closest to the heart and plunges the point in between them. His heart bursts like a tomato crushed on the sidewalk. She hears a faint rattle that soon stops.

It's not finished. Her panties stained with her virginal blood. No matter what, she must find them. She gropes for a long time in the dark and finally smells them under the rough cloth covering the body.

But where to dispose of them? If they are found in a flower bed they will be turned over to the investigators and will be handled by the thick hands of the police. She'd rather not think about what might come after. She wanders up and down the paths like a sick animal and stumbles on a wooden object: a cart full of leaves and branches. Pulling her sleeve up to the shoulder, she dives her hand into the decomposing mass and buries the ball of monogrammed silk at the very bottom.

She runs away, but a few steps farther along she discovers a well. She holds back in distress, wavering for a minute. Blood drips from her fingers. She returns to the cart and, digging her arm in again, rummages among the rot, recovers the panties, runs to the well, and hurls them down. On their way, the panties, unfolding, look like a pink flare.

She re-enters the palace, climbs the secret staircase, and pauses in a small toilet to clean up. She inspects her nightgown and bathrobe: there are traces of humidity but no suspect stains. Dried, powdered, and perfumed, her soul darkened by so many rash actions, she again reaches the nuptial chamber where yet another duty awaits.

"You took so long, *mi amor*," he says. "I began to be afraid."

"For us to be as one," she replies, trying to put him off the scent. Her king does not answer. He is thinking.

Oh! How she would like, how she would like to chase away these clouds of thought before they blacken his mind! How she would like to whisper in his ear the simple words: It's for you! For you, my king, my beloved! For you that I gave myself to that beastly human being! To spare you, by way of redemption, the plight of the initial penetration and to ease your way through the narrowness of the passage this first time. Ah! I don't wish to be guilty of the sin of pride, but does there exist in history a queen willing to commit such a sacrifice for her king?

Flinging off her bathrobe, she slips between the sheets and waits for her king to undress her completely.

"Oh! But you're all cold!" he cries out, uneasy once more.

"There was an open window," she says.

"A window? Where?"

"W-win . . . a window," she says, her voice dying out. "Oh . . ."

"My beauty," he murmurs, trembling.

"My most beautiful."

He gets up to check the clock for the third time. He cannot go back to sleep. It is not six o'clock and yet in his mind, it's brighter than a beach at noon. His eyes ache, his head aches. His body does not feel happily relaxed.

In certain women, there is no sign. Or almost no sign, is what the doctor said.

Almost no sign. He tries to imagine what that "almost no sign" means.

The sun shines a golden sliver on the wall at six thirty. She stirs and stretches. He imprisons her in his arms. Eyes shut, she swings toward him and then disentangles herself.

"I'll be back . . ."

She hurries toward the door. As soon as he hears her slippers lightly touching the floor, he turns backs the sheet and coverlet and examines the bottom sheet. Nothing. Stains, but not the ones he is looking for. Only his, pale, pearly green. *Nada.*

She returns, climbs into bed, slides toward him, and comes close. Without a word, he takes her again in a wild fury. He lashes out at her and penetrates into her very depths with rage. Because he is the king.

Edited by
Ruth Greenstein

Produced by
Wilsted & Taylor
Publishing Services

Copy editing
Melody Lacina

Design and composition
Yvonne Tsang

Proofreading
Nancy Evans

Printing and binding
Thomson-Shore, Inc.